# Branding for Real

Straight talking essays that help you build your brand.

By Lynn M. Parker

ISBN: 978-1-4507-5829-1



This book was printed in the United States of America.

To order additional copies of this book, contact:
Amazon Corporation
www.amazon.com
1-866-216-1072

# Contents

# Introduction

# Branding for Real

I hate the "branding" word. That's because it sounds so daunting, so abstract, with many meanings. Does it mean your company's logo? Your look and feel? Your name? The promise you deliver? The experience customers have with you? Or does it encompass all your customer touchpoints?

Despite its many meanings, for me, there is no other word that more clearly denotes the interface between company and consumer and the subsequent relationships—whether good or bad—that are created. In brand relationships, like any other relationship, you control only your half. That being said, it's important to control what you can control, to build trust in the relationship through authentic experiences, and foster an opportunity for people to engage with your brand by connecting with them on both a logical and emotional level.

In this compilation of essays, most of which were originally published by womenentrepreneur.com, I try to bring the abstract and unwieldy notion of "branding" to a level where companies of all sizes and types can understand its power and how to use it in their everyday lives. That's why this book is called "Branding for Real"—it has real ideas that real people can put into action today. Really.

Branding for Real includes ideas for articulating, building and living your company's brand, both online and off, and is divided into three sections for easier skimming: general thoughts on branding, digital branding (because it has its own unique challenges), and living the brand—implementing it through your employees.

So if you're looking for down-to-earth, practical advice on how "branding" can influence and improve your reality, you'll love Branding for Real. And even if you're not a fan of reality, you'll find it easier to cope with when you take this book's lessons to heart. Enjoy!

# Part One

# General Thoughts on Branding

How do you create a brand? How do you sustain it? What are the levers in making sure your company's value shows up for the market?

These are the types of questions these essays explore. The common thread that runs between them: consistently differentiate yourself now and over time, it's what the market wants and needs. If you demonstrate your unique value, they'll get it and if they like it, they'll hop on your bandwagon, become your brand's champion and help you deliver more of it.

# 1

# The Power of the "Early Win" in Defining a Brand

The best brands are different—they really stick out. They give you reasons to buy or engage that are different from the competition. You may look at tablets from many vendors, but you crave the elegant design of an iPad. You may fly any airline, but you appreciate the flight attendant humor at Southwest. You may stay at a variety of hotels, but when you get a warm cookie when you check in at Doubletree Inn, you feel comforted. You may buy shoes many places, but look forward to reading the Zappos employee blog as they tell stories of above and beyond service. Those are all brand-defining experiences for their respective companies.

So what is the first way prospects and customers know that your company or product is different? Are you thinking about your differentiation from an "early win" perspective, that is, are you making a statement or delivering an experience that tells the story of your brand right off the bat?

This early win is important because it sets the stage for customer expectations and beliefs going forward. This is particularly true today, as constant access to the digital world means we are always plugged into a world of knowledge and people that are rewriting the rules for buying and selling, loyalty and recommendation.

In this environment, effectively branding your company means you have to move from "the message" to "the experience." So what experience will most clearly distill your brand difference and win you a role in your customers' lives? That's the one you should focus on first—the early win that wows your customers while bringing your brand into clear definition.

So if you are airline Spanair, you might demonstrate your unique brand by giving presents to all your passengers who flew Christmas Eve, delivered in brightly wrapped packages with their luggage on the carousel—and share that video online so others could experience it too. Or if you're Salal Credit Union, whose brand is around being invested in your financial health, you might have financial education, debt consulting and financial planning services prominently displayed on your home page. Or if you're coffee roaster/retailer Zoka, which defines its brand as "coffee as ritual," you put coffee roasters in each of your retail outlets and run "cupping" workshops to train people in how to taste coffee.

I bet if you looked at the current ways people experience your brand, either through your website, your customer service, or other digital or face-to-face touchpoints, you might find that they do not lead customers and prospects to the right conclusions. Given your differentiation, what would be your ideal brand-defining experience? And what early win can you put out there to tell the story of your brand in a way that people get it quickly? That's the place to focus.

# 2

# Top Five Branding Mistakes

## Engaging in any one of these could sabotage your brand.

In my 25 years as a branding consultant, I've seen companies make major branding mistakes, some real doozies. One company wanted to tout itself as the most innovative, even though it spent zero dollars on research and development. Another acquired a well-respected competitor and then immediately changed its name, leaving millions of dollars worth of good will on the table. Those are obvious offenses. Many other companies make all-too-common--subtle yet avoidable--mistakes that sap the value right out of their brands. Here are five I would caution against.

### MISTAKE ONE: EQUATING BRANDING WITH COMMUNICATIONS

Yes, branding includes communications. But if your branding strategy is all about messaging and advertising and nothing about business strategy or people, then you won't be able to deliver on your communications. If you have lousy customer service, telling people it's great will only drive customers away faster. But investing in training and infrastructure to improve service will enable you to market your great service and still look yourself in the mirror. As more information about companies and products is available online, a great company and product are your brand's only defense.

## MISTAKE TWO: BRANDING ON PRICE

Don't do it. Basing your brand on your low price is a race to the bottom—and someone will always beat you there. Even if your prices are the same as your competitors' prices, you need to give clients compelling reasons beyond price to buy from you. The difference between the product offered by Morton Salt and a supermarket's house brand? Not much. The difference in pricing? Fourteen percent. That margin is due to how well Morton has built up the intangible parts of its brand. Establish trust with your customers, and you can breathe a lot easier when the newest competitor undercuts your price.

## MISTAKE THREE: CHANGING YOUR PROMISE

Like a dog sniffing at a fire hydrant, every time a new marketing vice president is brought into a company, there's a risk she'll try to change the brand, or put her mark on it. While your brand promise should be relevant and up-to-date, making a wholesale change from, say, being the educational leader to being the innovation leader will only confuse your market.

Are you ready to change your tagline or logo? Companies get tired of their own marketing way before the market does.

(You live with it day in and day out. They see it only once in a while.) Remember when Jack in the Box killed off its clown? Customer sentiment brought it back, but the company was smart enough to do so in an updated way, with the ping-pong-headed CEO. Whatever you do, don't let your visual brand identity and messaging force changes in your brand promise (see Mistake No. 1).

## MISTAKE FOUR: OVERPROMISING

The least expensive way to brand yourself is to have your customers do it for you. How do you get them to become evangelists? By underpromising and overdelivering. Fight the temptation to sound better than you are: Promise what you can deliver, then do it to the nth degree. Are you the fastest? Then don't give customers a long voice-mail message to listen to before they can act. Are you the friendliest? Don't let your employees bad-mouth clients behind their backs. Are you the coolest? Then make sure your lobby looks awesome and has wow power.

Alongside this advice, I recommend that you focus your brand message—don't try to be all things to all people. Figure out the most compelling part of your promise and build that up, rather than try to communicate 10 different elements of your brand promise.

## MISTAKE FIVE: ME-TOO BRANDING

I can't tell you how many entrepreneurs have said, "If I only get x percent of the market, I'll be rich." You have to give consumers a compelling reason to give you their business to get that percentage. You can't expect to siphon off business from the market leader without a substantive reason. Don't try to be like other companies: Be yourself. There will be a subsegment of the market that likes what you do better than what the market leader does, and that's the percentage of the market you can skim off. Instead of emulating competitors, be different. If you're competing against Starbucks, zig when it zags. Make your décor unique; encourage customers to play board games; roast beans on site; have coffee tasting parties. Get your own buzz on.

Steer clear of these mistakes, and you'll be well on your way to branding nirvana—being known for your compelling and differentiated value.

# 3

# Vitamin Brand

## You'll stay healthy by reinforcing your brand promise in everything you do.

Most of us are looking for the magic pill to keep business flowing in the down economy. Sadly, that magic pill doesn't exist. But the equivalent of exercising and eating right can be applied to business: I call it Vitamin Brand. Taken regularly, the hypothetical Vitamin Brand can help you weather the economic downturn. Here are five ways Vitamin Brand can work for you:

### TAKE VITAMIN BRAND TO MAKE YOUR DIFFERENCE BIGGER

Branding is about meaningful differentiation and focus. Since so many people are hunkering down instead of getting out there, you have a great opportunity to increase awareness of your differentiation. Look for low-cost or no-cost ways either to deliver more of your unique benefit or communicate that benefit to others. For example, Group Health Cooperative is demonstrating its brand of innovation for better health by taking a leading role in the current health-care reform conversation. CEO Scott Armstrong, who has been invited to the White House twice to discuss health-care reform, is championing electronic health records, integrated payment and delivery systems, evidence-based decisions, preventive and primary care, and universal coverage.

## ENSURE THAT YOUR ONLINE PRESENCE EXUDES VITAMIN BRAND

Your entire web strategy needs to reflect your brand, from applications, user interface, navigation and content to audience gateways. You can have a great promise and deliver great value, but if your website looks and acts like everyone else's, you've lost an opportunity. If your company is branded as the friendliest, then have a friendly website. If you're the most innovative, have the most innovative one.

## LOOK FOR MORE CUSTOMERS LIKE THOSE ALREADY TAKING YOUR VITAMIN BRAND

Branding is about aligning your value with your customers—moving them from awareness through preference, loyalty and on to commitment by demonstrating how your approach and their needs are in perfect harmony. This means that for a specific set of customers—your most loyal, evangelizing ones—you provide value unlike anyone else. By figuring out who your best customers are and specifically what they value about you, you'll have a blueprint for getting more loyal customers. At Parker LePla, for example, we discovered that nonprofits appreciated our long-term, values-based approach, so we grew a nonprofit part of our practice, with messaging, marketing and focus on that subset.

## INCREASE YOUR VITAMIN BRAND-BASED PROMOTIONS

Money-off promotions are a tried-and-true way to kick-start sales; but make sure they reinforce your brand. For example, Hyundai is offering to let people return cars if they lose their job. Very on-brand, very promotional.

## SHARE HOW VITAMIN BRAND HAS HELPED

It doesn't cost money to think up brand-based stories and talk about them. If part of your brand is alternative thinking, come up with anecdotes demonstrating that quality, then tell them to your employees and have them share their own stories. Your employees are your best brand ambassadors. If you get them to tell their friends and neighbors about your company's products and services through the lens of brand promise, then you're employing the cheapest and most trusted marketing around: word-of-mouth. Create a culture of storytelling at your organization, so that every voice is reinforcing your brand difference.

So no magic pill—just advice to look long-term, continue to improve and reinforce your promise in everything you do.

# 4

# The Power of Brand Architecture

## Effective brand architecture makes it easy for customers to purchase products that meet their needs.

Chances are, if your company has more than one product line, you're confusing your customers. That's because most company's product brands grow in organic ways that don't fall into neat categories customers can understand. The way a company organizes its brands often bears little resemblance to what matters to customers. Like a house needs a blueprint before it can be built, your brands might need an architectural structure so you can build more customer loyalty.

For brand architecture to be effective, it must be structured from the customer's point of view, not the company's. Organizing a company's brand architecture as an exact duplicate of its organizational chart won't help deliver a compelling brand experience. The best architecture makes it simple and easy for customers to understand the value and purchase the products that best meet their needs. For example, let's say a company is set up divisionally with hardware and software divisions, and markets its services that way. If customers expect to have the two bundled, it will create an additional barrier to customer purchase and may stymie business growth.

So what's your company's brand architecture? Figuring this out is worth any amount of time and energy. Clear brand architecture will bear fruit in several ways:

- You'll be able to better align and meet your business goals by focusing your efforts.
- You'll be able to leverage your assets and resources to create synergy among product offerings.
- You'll know which products fit within your model.
- You'll know how to organize and name new products so customers recognize their value.
- You'll get ideas for new product offerings that meet current market needs.
- You'll have created a clear, consistent and simple way for customers to understand your offerings and their unique value.

## WHAT IS BRAND ARCHITECTURE?

A company's brand architecture determines several things:

- How you relate your brands to each other
- How you talk about the complementary value of

your corporate and product brands

- How many brands you offer
- What products fit and where
- Whether to use evocative or descriptive names

One effective brand architecture is the branded house, where there is a master brand (usually the company name), sub-brands (product lines) and descriptive products, customer service or program names. There may also be ingredient brands, such as Intel's Inside, or GE's Ecomagination.

The opposite of a branded house is a house of brands, like that of Procter & Gamble, where you don't buy the P&G name; the meaning is held within individual brands such as Pringles, Zest and Duracell.

For instance, IBM focuses on its master brand—IBM—and gives its product brands a lesser role in its marketing. The master brand is the primary named brand that holds a shared value across all products. Honda is a master brand that stands for reliability and excellent handling—this is true whether you buy a Civic or an Accord. A sub-brand is a product brand, typically with an evocative name, that is always in relationship to a master brand. Honda Civic, for example, for those who want a smaller car or a lower-priced offering. A descriptive product/service name explains the basic value of the product/service without explanation, such as Honda Civic Sedan, which means it has four doors. An ingredient brand is a named brand that provides supporting value to other brands, often expressed as an icon, such as Honda Civic Sedan with XM Satellite radio. The ingredient is not the reason to buy the brand, but it is an added feature or benefit that enhances its value.

How do you figure out which products should be sub-brands, with real, branded names vs. merely descriptive names? It's a judgment call, weighing the importance of the product, the target market and the relationship of the product to the parent brand. If you have too many names, it becomes a code that customers have to figure out. Descriptive names might not build a strong enough product line.

Ingredient brands emphasize aspects of a brand's value or a new trend that may not be well understood but is important for the future of a market. Ecomagination is one example of how a complex and hard-to-define concept, sustainability, can be attached to an evocative symbol that acts as a shorthand for many supporting ideas. This symbol then becomes something customers use to make product choices. Which would you rather choose, a sustainable product that you have good feelings about (strongly reinforced by Ecomagination) or a product that doesn't have this pedigree?

So what's your company's brand architecture? Is your brand house in order, or do you need a new blueprint for growth and customer loyalty?

# 5

# Don't Dilute Your Brand

## Doing so can confuse customers. Stick to your brand focus, and be the best at what you do.

The problem with entrepreneurs is that they like to grow things. This may not seem like a problem, but if the growth doesn't tell a story, if it isn't focused around a single idea, the customer can get confused.

Here's an example: A successful tattoo-removal company decides to branch out into other skin-care services, such as dermabrasion and chemical peels. That may be fine, depending on the company's strategic role in the market. Is the company known as a place you go to look your best for work? Then more skin-care services may make sense. Is it known as a place where your physical self keeps up with your changing identity? Then a more on-brand direction for new services may be in plastic surgery or tattoo creation. But adding services just because you can is a recipe for customer confusion.

This is what I see all the time: An organization starts with a focused idea, achieves a modicum of success with it and then starts looking for new ways to grow. It grows through related services and products, builds new divisions and starts to create silos. Unmanaged by a single brand principle, a company's growth can become diluted. The natural tendency is to lose brand focus and soon end up meaning everything, hence nothing. And it doesn't necessarily take a lot of growth to get there.

When companies create their strategic plans, what they use as their compass can make a big difference. It's all very well to be opportunistic, but you would be much more powerful if you figured out what was at the heart of your value, built on that and became the best at that in the world. That's the way Apple, Volvo, Google, Zappos and other strong brands got to the top.

Losing one's way happens more often than companies like to admit. A company that is always creating new products, but whose products don't tell a coherent story, is ripe for losing customers. General Motors, Tully's and Eddie Bauer all have that in common. You see, we're all pattern seekers: We look for and find patterns in everything we come in contact with, whether it's our spouse's behavior or which route is best for our daily commute. And in the absence of a coherent pattern, from our spouses or the companies we do business with, we find confusion, frustration and, ultimately, avoidance.

Steering by the light of your company's brand is the easiest way to ensure focus and brand coherence. Questions CEOs should ask themselves during strategic planning are:

- What can we add, change or eliminate to further our brand's promise?
- What is the most important thing we can do to reinforce our core brand's meaning in the mind of our customers?
- Are there any parts of our company that are off-brand?

A master practitioner of this approach to focus is Volvo. The reason you think "safety" when you think Volvo is a long-term result of the company's unending focus on it. That focus is manifested by its R&D efforts; by safety innovations that are added before the government requires them; by a website called "Volvo Saved My Life Club" with customer stories; by a tagline that reinforces safety; and, of course, by ongoing marketing communications that stress safety. The result is that Volvo owns "safety" in the customer's mind, and that's worth a lot.

Now, what if Volvo decided to create a line of cars that were sporty, but not safe? The customer would be confused, and confusion doesn't lead to purchases.

So what's at the heart of your brand promise? Are you steering by it, or is it time to refocus your company's efforts?

# 6

# Build Your Brand for Longevity

## Use these 7 strategies to make your brand sustainable.

It's a useful exercise to anthropomorphize. So close your eyes and envision your company's brand as a living, breathing thing. Got the picture in your mind?

I hope you see a unique being with its own character, personality, purpose and behaviors. And like any living thing, it must be cared for to reach its potential and be a sustainable brand. Here are best practices to grow and tend your brand for longevity:

### STRATEGIZE

As we move in sophistication from thinking about brands as logos to brands as experiences, you must use your brand promise to drive business planning. This means that the most important question you can ask is, "What should we do this year to increase our brand value difference in the market?"

Your brand must be your primary strategy driver, not just something you communicate. You must be committed to your brand's value over time and invest in actions that deliver more of your brand promise to the market. So if your brand is about being the best partner, for example, dedicate a portion of your annual planning process to shoring up current partnerships and identifying ways you can be a better partner at all levels.

## CONSISTIFY

OK, I made up that word. But the idea still applies: Make sure your visual and verbal brand speaks with one voice, and that your customer touchpoints all deliver on your key value. It's good practice to put all your customer-facing materials on a table and see if you get one message or many.

## UPDATE SPARINGLY

It's OK to refresh your look and feel. You can come out with new ad campaigns. Just make sure that the heart of your brand—its DNA—doesn't change over time. What you can change is the additional ways you demonstrate your brand in your actions, products, programs and communications. Change how you say it, not what you say.

## GET IT OUT THERE

You can't secure customer preference, loyalty or commitment levels of engagement for your brand without the first step: awareness. Look for low- or no-cost ways to get your brand in front of prospects. As Chinese philosopher Lao Tzu put it, "A journey of a thousand miles begins with a single step."

## LOCALIZE

If your brand shows up in different countries or regions, make sure 70 percent of your brand's value, meaning and personality stays consistent, while you change 30 percent of it to match the specific culture. Check out Apple's ads in Japan, the United Kingdom and the U.S. on YouTube if you want to see a master of the art of localization.

## CONTEXTUALIZE

Look for places and times for your brand to show up where its value will be most appreciated. For example, airports are a desirable demographic for Wi-Fi networks. There's a captive audience of passengers who are stuck there and bored.

## BENCHMARK

Ideally, you should measure the strength and content of your brand yearly, so you know what pieces need shoring up and what you're doing well. You can do this via a web-based survey. For example, if your brand is predicated on innovation, and your innovative scores dip, then you know a key foundational part of your brand needs more attention.

Brands are not static—they change through time. The key is knowing what should be updated and what needs to stay consistent so that your value grows. Managing your brand through time will make it sustainable.

# 7

# Bringing Brands Alive through Storytelling

## Storytelling crystallizes your brand into a size and shape that people understand.

"Once upon a time." Are any other four words in the English language quite so evocative? Humans are hard-wired to tell and listen to stories, from the time we're born to the time we die. Stories are how we share information, impart wisdom and convey meaning. It's baked in.

What does this have to do with branding? Everything.

One of the main tools organizations and customers have for communicating a brand's value is telling stories. Think about a time you had a bad experience with a brand. Did you keep it to yourself, or did you tell the story of how [name deleted upon advice of counsel] truly messed up an opportunity with you by losing your reservation and then trying to make it your fault? Or think about the time you used a Nordstrom personal shopper; think of how great an experience it was and how it made you feel special. Or consider how Tony Hsieh, CEO of Zappos, is always talking about his company's culture and giving examples of how it aims for awesome customer service.

Stories are how we talk about and identify brands, so companies need to learn how to tell their own stories and turn their employees into storytellers. How? First, you have to train people in the art and science of storytelling. Every brand has a set of elements you can use to create your own stories. The first element is values. What is the key theme you want to get across so that people understand what drives your organization?

Next, you need to tell an anecdote expressing that theme. It has to include people, actions and beliefs as a result of those actions. Every story needs an arc—a setup, some conflict or challenge and a resolution. Here's an example:

We really want working at Parker LePla to be satisfying for our employees. (theme) So we have what we call the "root canal test." (setup) This test is a result of something that happened early in our formation when we had one client (people) that made up a high percentage of our total book of business. Unfortunately, it was kind of an abusive relationship. The client would berate us, make us feel bad and try to get out of paying its bills. Because we were a new company, with few other clients, we thought we had to take it. (conflict)

One day, as my partner and I (people) were walking to the client's office, he said, "I'd rather have a root canal than go to this meeting." I said, "In that case, let's fire them. Life is too short to hate your clients." (beliefs and anecdote) So we did (actions), even though it meant that hitting profitability took a few months longer. Now, our employees know that we're serious about their well-being and that work should be fun. We apply the root canal test to problematic clients to determine if we want them or not, and we have fired clients that failed the test—albeit rarely. Today, we have only great clients—ones that appreciate us and that work in partnership with us. (resolution and theme)

That story is much more effective at informing our employees about how we look at the world and our value system than a generic statement about trying to create a great working environment or striving to find clients that map to our values.

Stories can change employee behavior or explain management decisions to employees in a way that policies and memos can't. One client, whose brand focuses on "Guiding Customers through Complex Printing Decisions," tells stories that demonstrate how it helps customers figure out innovative ways to save money. This helps our client's customers understand its brand, but it also influences employee behavior, so that employees, too, look for more ways to save the customers money. Another client, a sleep clinic whose brand centers on "Taking Sleep Seriously," tells stories of people whose lives changed once they solved their sleep issues. Yet another client, a consulting firm whose brand is around uplifting project management to a new concept of "Program Ownership," uses its sales presentation to tell stories that demonstrate the difference between project management and program ownership, and why clients appreciate the latter.

The story crystallizes the communication into a size and shape that we as humans have evolved to understand. Stories bring abstract concepts to life and are the easiest way both to train employees to live the brand and to tell prospects why they want your brand.

Start telling more stories, and see if it doesn't make a difference.

# 8

# Accomplish the Impossible: Choose a Name

## Here are some tips to help you create a memorable company name and brand.

Naming is practically impossible—ask anyone who's done it. Why is naming so hard? I can think of three reasons:

1. Names are subjective.
2. No one ever likes a name at first blush (or can imagine what meaning it will hold in the future).
3. All the good ones are already taken.

On a basic brand level, your name is your top-level identifier and the first differentiator in a crowded space, so it's important to get it right.

So even though it's a seemingly impossible task, how can you name (or rename) a company or product and be successful?

First, know what you want your name to do. Should it:

- Stand out from competitors' names?
- ID your key benefit?
- Roll off the tongue?
- Suggest an idea?

Creating the criteria for name selection is arguably the most important part of a successful naming process, because you can generate alternatives that meet that criteria, and you have a way of judging names beyond "I like it" or "I don't like it."

Whether you like a name is irrelevant. Do you think Google, as a name, wowed the venture capitalists when first presented? Did Starbucks show up as a brilliant nom de guerre upon first sighting? I don't think so. Remember, you build meaning into a name over time.

Second, lean toward memorable names over descriptive ones. New entrepreneurs often are attracted to descriptive names because they want customers to know what they do. But your name shouldn't do that heavy lifting, and it will typically be in context when customers see it. A descriptive name is generic: It does advertising for your whole industry, not just for you. And it's hard to remember.

What's easier to remember: Exquisite Events or Whistling Rabbits? Print Management or SharpDog? In each case, the new name evokes thoughts, images and feelings, leading to memorability. Your goal is for your target audience to notice the name, be intrigued by it and then remember it. A name that stands out is the way to do this. A fun, interesting name will be a better vessel for brand meaning than something flatter and more generic.

Finally, use a proven process for name generation and selection. At my agency, we start with the criteria and brainstorm literally hundreds of options. We use a variety of techniques and launching points, such as coined morphemes (making up new prefixes and suffixes) and Latin dictionaries, then select the best for vetting. We screen for such things as preliminary trademark and URL availability, internet search results and foreign language meanings, ending up with 10 to 15 strong names for client presentation. (Ideally, we would run these names by a trademark lawyer even before presentation, but real-world budgets usually don't allow for that level of due diligence.)

The fun begins with the selection process. Because it is so easy to ruin a name for someone else via an idle comment, we start the process with a silent, individual selection process. (Imagine what would have happened to Starbucks if someone had said, "Doesn't that name remind people how expensive our coffee is?" Or, before everyone had a chance to think through the name "Amazon," someone said "Won't people think of one-breasted women warriors when they are buying books online?") We hand out information about the names in application, in competitive context and with all the vetting data we've compiled.

Only after each team member has voted on his or her top three names do we open up the conversation for discussion. We focus only on the top five vote getters, since there's no value in spending time on names that didn't pass muster. People who like a specific name sell the others on why they like it, and we run each name against the criteria from the beginning of the process.

From this process, usually a group can come to consensus on which name(s) to send on to legal for approval. Don't neglect this last step—a good trademark lawyer can save you many headaches (current and future).

So good luck doing the impossible. And may your name be memorable.

# 9

# How to Turn Negative Branding Positive

## Politicians do it all the time. Take 'Obamacare,' a once-derisive name the Democrats are now owning.

It started when right-wing pundits decided to attack the 2009 health-care reform effort with a pejorative: "Obamacare." This term became shorthand for all the potential drawbacks of the wide-sweeping reform legislation—reminding people that a not-so-popular president was behind it.

But recently something shifted. Taking a lesson from other attacked groups, such as the gay activists who embrace the formerly negative label "queer," the left wing has now taken the once-negative term "Obamacare" and made it its own. I heard a left-wing pundit on the radio use the term, which surprised me. Yet I shouldn't have been surprised: It's a common strategy to embrace negativity to take away its power.

So what's in a name? Is it a good strategy to appropriate the name Obamacare? Or is using the Obamacare label a decision that will continue to carry negative connotations? No matter what your opinion about health-care reform, taking away the sting of name-calling by referring to yourself with the same name can be effective.

Naming something is so hard precisely because our opinion of whether a name is good changes with time, typically from dislike to like. At first, names are empty vessels that we fill with meaning. And we usually hate them, because they don't mean anything to us. Even the names we think are great ones, such as Google or Kodak, were at their start just sounds, devoid of all the associations we now bring to them. When Shakespeare said a rose would smell as sweet if it were called something else, he was talking about branding. He was talking about how actions and communications fill a name with meaning, not the other way around. The infusion process takes time, which is why the left owning the term Obamacare is like voting in Chicago: It's best done early and often.

Another example of someone in politics taking a negative and turning it into a positive is President Bush, with his new book. Derided as "the decider," Bush has titled his new book Decision Points. A classically trained marketer might suggest a name that doesn't remind people of the negative label. A social-brand marketer might see instead the need to base the book's title upon what people are already thinking, thereby providing additional meaning and becoming part of the process that determines value. A book title that refutes the Decider pejorative will generate more buzz than one with a lofty and abstract title.

This is a good example of how brands have evolved from a

unidirectional process—a corporation broadcasting to the masses—into social brands, where the consumer shares in the ownership of the brand's meaning. President Obama didn't put the health-care legislation out there as Obamacare, but now that the community knows that moniker, he is wise to own it and share in its future definition. Similarly, President Bush couldn't take back his "I am the decider" comment, but he can make it his own and provide a more positive spin and context.

The shift in claiming labels points to the sea change that is happening in marketing: Things are moving from marketing to conversation, from telling to listening, from image to authenticity. It will require new ways of thinking for businesses and—sometimes—embracing the negative so you can add your voice to the positive. Are you ready?

# Part Two

# Digital Branding

Now that the Internet has turned all the rules upside down and sped up the rate of change by about a bazillion times, what does that mean for your brand? People won't watch your YouTube videos, visit your website, read your blogs, comment on your Facebook page or download your apps if they don't immediately get value. From your website architecture to your content strategy to SEO, your brand's digital experience needs to align with your off-line experiences and engage users through differentiated and relevant experiences. Read this section and act fast, because by the time you're done, there will already be new digital implications for your brand to consider.

# 10

# Translating your Brand to the Web

## More important than looking good, it must clearly communicate the value of your business.

For many online companies, such as Expedia or Evite, the web is their brand experience because they offer online services through online channels. For other organizations, web presence is more like "brochureware"—in other words, a static marketing channel for real-world products and services. But whether your product is virtual or requires a warehouse and a forklift, the key is how you demonstrate and show your brand promise online.

As the front door to your prospects, your website becomes your brand's face. From the moment they land on your home page, visitors make snap judgments about the value you provide, how you're different from competitors and whether they feel an emotional connection to your brand. So it's important to consider how well your web presence communicates your value.

Smart business owners get this, but they often respond to this imperative by spending a lot of time on their site's design, colors and images. That's a good start, but design is only part of a prospect's online experience.

Equally important are:

- The type of content you have
- How the content is organized for each of your target users
- How it drives them to a deeper level of engagement with you
- How well it delivers on your brand promise.

For small businesses with limited resources, the website is crucial because it has to do so much work. It acts as a community outreach, sales, marketing and workflow management tool. And if you believe—as I do—that everything you do and say as a company makes up your brand promise, then your site must reflect your brand through and through. Otherwise, you'll leave customers wondering which experience they'll get the next time they call.

## WHAT DOES THIS MEAN TO YOU?

Before you hire a designer, start by thinking of your site as an extension of your business strategy rather than just a line item in your marketing budget. And the best way to bridge from your brand to your site is with a web strategy.

A web strategy provides intention and discipline to your website development process. It ties your brand and business goals for the year to content development, management and measurement strategies that guide the brand experience you provide on the web. What goes into a web strategy? Here's an outline:

- It keeps tabs on your user profiles, allowing you to dive more deeply into who your users are and what they need from your site.
- It determines what the competitive landscape looks like.
- It audits stakeholder requirements.
- It maps out exactly what type of experience your site should deliver.
- It figures out what you should measure and how you should measure it (both via offline measurement tactics and online analytics), based on your goals and objectives.

In a nutshell, your web strategy is a lot like a website owner's manual, giving you all the tools you need to build, adapt and manage your online brand experience.

So stop and think about the front door to your company's brand experience. Make sure it looks good. But more important, make sure it opens into your organization's promise and creates customer champions.

# 11

# Customers Want Experiences, Not Products

## Marketing is no longer a one-way game. Be prepared to hold a dialogue with customers.

Have you ever woken up in a hotel room in a strange city and couldn't figure out where you were? That feeling of disorientation is common to those of us who received classic training in the art of marketing. Here we were, going along with our messaging matrices, marketing mixes, communication strategies and media plans when—Pow!—Web 2.0 and social media came along and changed the landscape, practically overnight.

Suddenly, traditional approaches to branding and marketing aren't as effective. People aren't looking for products anymore; they are seeking experiences, ways to engage and be engaged with, to be heard. This changes the marketing game from a one-way dissemination of information to a multi-directional dialogue that seeks to build relationships—where sales may be one outcome, but certainly not the only one.

In this confusing world, your brand is more important than ever. That's because the best brands already know they deliver a unique customer experience, which is what customers are looking for. The good news is that there are many more ways to engage with customers and prospects (and their social networks) online. The not-so-good news is that you have to manage your brand even more carefully as a result. It's now about building an online experience that supports your offline brand efforts while creating an environment for ongoing listening, conversation and engagement with your audiences.

The place to start is with your website. Make it the online hub for your brand because, after all, it's now your front door. Everything you do online—advertising, e-mail marketing, social networking, social media engagement—should include the call to action to go to your website so you can control the experience and move visitors up the engagement scale. Once the visitors arrive, you need to pay off the promise. To do this, you must stop looking at your website as an online brochure and start looking at it as an experience you want people to have with you, your products, your people—your brand. What do you want them to do when they are there? How do you want them to feel? What do you want them to say to their friends about it?

Developing an online experience that engages and builds relationships starts with a well-informed strategy. First, you need to understand your users and the value you bring to them. One part is knowing who they are, what their goals are, what motivates them, what needs they have and how they behave online. The other part is really understanding why they would choose you—what do they truly value about you? When you understand these things implicitly, you can map out what kind of experience they want to have with you online and then design toward it.

We call this "experience mapping." It looks at each of your unique user groups and maps out where they are online (what sites, what search engines, what social networks, etc.), what paths they would take to get to your site, what they would do there and the choices they would make as they navigate through the site. This is a key step in developing your strategy because it points to all of the important components of online experience design: your social media presence, your online marketing presence, your keyword buys and your website. Someone who has done this step many times will be able to create an experience map quickly; but you can do it yourself if you understand your audiences well.

Your online strategy helps to inform the navigation style you choose, your content strategy, the language you use on your site, the design aesthetic you employ, the interactive features and more. When you design with your users and their needs and values in mind, your online brand becomes a destination and a useful tool in their lives—just where you want to be to build strong relationships with them, the kind that drive sales over the long term.

Experiences are what make brands. That doesn't change whether you are providing that experience on the phone, in your store, on your website or via Facebook. The more seamless you make that experience, the stronger your relationships will be.

# 12

# Create a Wise Web Strategy

## Follow these 6 steps to create an action plan that will deliver your brand promise online.

How do you ensure that your website's architecture, content, navigation and overall experience are both delivering on your brand promise and aligning with your business goals? In this chapter, I'll list the six steps needed to create your own web strategy.

### STEP ONE: ARTICULATE YOUR UNIQUE VALUE

Make sure you understand the content of your brand promise before starting a website project. At the very least, identify what you do better, how you're different and whom you're targeting.

### STEP TWO: REVIEW WHAT YOU'VE GOT

If you have an existing website, take a look at your current site analytics (Google Analytics is a great, free resource tracking tool). This will help you get a feel for who's using your site, what they're after and how they're finding their way to you. This can also serve as a baseline for helping you develop your website strategy, including your user personas (see Step 3), key objectives and measurement strategy.

## STEP THREE: GET TO KNOW YOUR AUDIENCE

Create a series of user profiles to help you better understand the needs, motivations and online behaviors of your target audiences. It's helpful to create actual personas that include a name and picture, their occupation, as well as a brief personal history to help you get into the users' mind-set and understand what information they'll be looking for, how they'll navigate through your site and how you can deliver the optimal experience. Start with the point of pain they are easing by visiting your site, and build from there.

## STEP FOUR: ASSESS THE COMPETITION

Develop a visual diagram to help you assess your top competitors. As you navigate through their sites, try to experience it as if you were each of your persona profiles and ask yourself:

- What's their brand promise?
- Are they delivering an on-brand experience?
- How are they positioning themselves in the market?
- Who do you think their target audiences are?
- What's the hierarchy of the content?

- Can you easily navigate through the site to find what you're looking for?
- What features do you appreciate?

## STEP FIVE: CREATE A WEB STRATEGY

The key to success: Align your website's infrastructure and objectives with your business goals through the development of a web strategy. Use your current analytics, your user personas and your competitive analysis to help devise a strategy. Ask yourself, what types of content will help you deliver on your brand promise and meet the needs of your users? Then create a list of the content you plan to include on your website. For example:

- Solutions offered
- Profiles/case studies
- Proprietary resources
- Blogs
- News and events
- Client testimonials
- Video, audio, flash tutorials or demos
- User-published content
- Feeds, links, newsletters
- Custom applications

Decide how you'll organize your site: Where will content live?

How will various items relate to one another? How will users navigate through the site? As you lay out this visual, ask yourself: What will people see when they land on the home page and how will they interact with the site from here on? Where will content live? Is the site delivering the experience users are expecting based on what we know about them?

I recommend creating a sketch of your home page to display how the real estate will be designated for each type of content, how the navigational style will influence the user's journey through the site and to demonstrate how you've translated your brand promise to the online experience. From there, create a site map (a visual layout of the site's architecture) to show how users will navigate through the site to find content.

## STEP SIX: CREATE A MEASUREMENT STRATEGY

Keep in mind that objectives need to be specific, measurable and attainable, and should always map back to your yearly business goals. If, for instance, one of your business goals is to increase new business leads, your web strategy needs to include the tactical measures to make that happen. That means:

- Make the contact form easy to fill out
- Provide an incentive for filling out the form
- Provide clear next steps for contact.

Limit yourself to five or six objectives; too many objectives become too hard to measure and attain.

Remember, a good website isn't determined by a flashy design; it's about communicating your distinct value by:

- Understanding your differentiated value
- Understanding who your users are
- Delivering valuable, organized content in a space that's easy to navigate
- Creating a site that fortifies your relationship with prospects and customers alike by driving deeper engagement.

# 13

# The ABCs of Social Branding

## Your online social interactions affect the perception of your brand, so make sure you're engaged.

Given the role social media plays in the world, you have to know how online social interactions are impacting perceptions about your company's brand.

The behaviors a company must engage in to build a social brand are different than those of traditional brand building, which was about broadcasting your message and living up to your brand promise through your products and services.

Customer relationships are far more multidimensional now. Social branding embraces listening, participation and engagement in online brand communities. This includes company-sponsored websites and social media, but it also includes being part of thousands of other communities, networks and face-to-face experiences where employees, customers and other interested parties talk about your company or topics related to what your company does.

For example, I can take part in the Apple community directly on the Apple-sponsored Facebook site. I can indulge my need for behind-the-scenes Apple news on the independent webzine Apple Matters. I can rave about my new iPod on my personal Facebook page, or I can read blogs written by others about their Apple experiences. In each of those activities, Apple's social brand is built, virtual brick by virtual brick.

## FROM TELLING TO TALKING

If traditional branding pushes opinions and information to customers, social branding, in contrast, is about encouraging information flows in every direction: between employees and customers, customers and customers, employees and employees, and influencers and everyone. Social branding goes well beyond receiving market information to engaging, networking and community building, one customer at a time.

By changing branding from a one-dimensional experience to a series of conversations, social branding turns the company—collectively and as individual employees—into participants finding ways to fuel meaningful conversations and evolve the brand. While your company will experience this as losing some control over the brand, the upside is a much more powerful and meaningful brand experience. A strong social brand builds preference through peer endorsements as well as positive product and company experiences. By creating this broad network, you will also build a defense and extended support team in times of crisis (think about all the loyal Toyota owners chatting on Facebook some months ago).

## BUILDING A BRAND COMMUNITY: TWO GREAT EXAMPLES

My Starbucks Idea is a great brand community-building example, where anyone can offer up suggestions for products or services from Starbucks, many of which actually get implemented. This collaboration with the customer is a great example of the company extending its brand promise to the web (of being the Third Place in people's lives, after home and work).

At an even more personal level, Comcast monitors Twitter for customer concerns and uses that information to advance product development efforts and solve problems. It has also taken Twitter mining to another level by responding to problems tweeted by customers. Comcast's brand promise is innovation and reliability. Monitoring Twitter allows it to be highly responsive to customer-service issues such as downtime. That improves reliability while also demonstrating that the company is tech-savvy.

Here are six key guidelines for building your social brand:

1. Recognize that the online brand community is something you influence but don't control.

2. Create strategies for building community around areas of interest, communicating your message and getting feedback from customers. This includes participating in conversations that aren't about your message and marketing, and leading new conversations based on what you hear people talking about.

3. Develop a set of employee guidelines (not rules!)

that include legal, etiquette and on-brand actions.

4. Train employees on the basics of being company brand ambassadors, including ways for them to tell their own stories about the brand.

5. Monitor the conversation. Track what people are talking about in your industry on existing as well as up-and-coming social media vehicles.

6. Experiment, and continuously improve.

# 14

# Does Social Media Drive Sales?

## Even if the answer is no, can you afford not to be present?

What's the relationship between social media and actual ring-the-cash-register, show-up-on QuickBooks results (not just engagement)?

That's the $64,000 question. From everything I've heard, that relationship is still elusive. According to a recent survey by SiriusDecisions and Visible Technologies, while 40 percent of companies are using social media to market their products, half of those can't show the impact of these efforts on their business. That's a lot of wasted time.

We can track engagement, awareness and consideration, but sales? That's not as clear. You can track the relationship of sales in time to postings on Facebook or Twitter, or you can track response to actual ads on Facebook or Twitter. But many social media tactics are designed to drive engagement, not that thing that keeps us in business—a purchase. In other words, unless you have a product or service you can market through discounting, a contest or another "act now" strategy, it's nearly impossible to measure direct impact.

Does the inability to track the relationship between social media efforts and sales mean there isn't one? No. The classic marketing model, where you move prospects from awareness through preference, purchase and loyalty, still applies. Social media can clearly influence the earlier stages of the marketing model—and without pouring prospects into your marketing funnel, you can't get sales out the bottom of it.

Whether it leads to more sales or not, everyone is moving to social media. Today, according to comScore, social media comprises 20 percent of all U.S. display ad impressions. Sixty percent of Americans use social media, and 85 percent of users believe a company should not only be present but also interact with its consumers via social media.

If you aren't employing social media these days, you are missing a huge population of people who are already engaged and are more likely—as well as more willing—to hear your message, which does equate to lost opportunities and potentially lost sales.

The mandate is clear. Your brand has to become a social brand, meaning that you use social media as a primary driver for building brand value. So how do you make sure the cycles you spend on social media pay off?

You're probably tired of hearing this from me, but it bears repeating: First, start with a strategy. Get clear about the online brand experience you wish to cultivate. Then drive that through social media into the communities where your customers, fans and influencers hang out. Tactics for building your social brand include:

- How you leverage website and social media experiences and turn your website into a hub for engagement
- How you engage employees to live your brand
- How you design products or services to facilitate engagement with your brand
- How your customers and others share their insights to build your brand's value
- How to measure all of this in ways that demonstrate bottom-line impact.

It's important to recognize that the online brand communities where your social brand lives aren't something your company can control—you share the task of building brand value with all other community members. You also can't control every employee post or comment, so you need to engage your employees as well as your customers and focus on influencing their behavior.

## BEST PRACTICES IN SOCIAL BRANDING

- Train employees on guidelines that include legal requirements and etiquette—guidelines, not rules.
- Build your culture and be clear on what authentic, on-brand actions and communications look

like so employees have content guidance.

- Include specific metrics that measure the success of your brand community within the social realm and how it contributes to internal culture-building and bottom-line results.
- Monitor and add up-and-coming social media vehicles to your social brand strategy.

Once you've clarified your social brand strategy, your online marketing strategy will become much, much clearer—and more effective. Bottom line: Does social media marketing actually improve your bottom line?

A 2008 BuzzLogic/Jupiter Research study of 2,000 online consumers found that blogs were a prime influencer of purchase decisions, with 50 percent of blog readers saying they found blogs useful for purchase information. Twenty-five percent of blog readers say they trust ads on a blog they read. Today, that's as close as we'll get to an answer.

But the truth is you can't afford to ignore your company's social brand, whether the relationship between social branding efforts and sales is one-to-one or not. It's a new cost of doing business, whether we like it or not. So get good at it.

# 15

# Tired of Social Media?

## If Social Media Fatigue Syndrome (SMFS) has you down, here's how to get over it.

If you're not a digital native, you're probably overwhelmed by the challenges of social media. And if you're like me, you're experiencing a touch of SMFS—social media fatigue syndrome. But there's a clear path to leveraging social media that promises—if not an immediate cure—management of the chronic condition.

The truth is, you can't afford SMFS. As one of the least expensive ways to promote your business, social media has a key role to play as part of your overall marketing mix. But more than that, it helps you do business differently. It can help you connect on a more personal level with your key prospects to raise awareness, develop deeper relationships, change perceptions and spread your message.

Don't apply it in isolation, though, because you'll waste a lot of time. Think about it as a tool to help you create a social brand—one that listens, engages and relates more closely to its customers to create greater brand champions. Implementing a successful social media strategy requires some strategic thinking and a clear plan. It also requires knowing what your brand promise is, so that you can live it online. Here are eight steps to follow to relieve SMFS.

## GET CLEAR ABOUT YOUR PURPOSE

Social media is . . . well, social. It's about building community, which means you have to earn the trust of those you want to interact with. Do you want to cultivate thought leadership or create a network of people who test and respond to your new ideas? You need to have a goal, whatever it is.

## SEEK OUT YOUR KEY AUDIENCES ONLINE AND, ONCE YOU FIND THEM, LISTEN

By visiting blogs, Twitter, Facebook and other key social media sites geared toward your industry, you can see the conversations people are having and gain insight into their current perceptions. In listening to their ideas, you'll find more ways to deliver value. Are they talking about your brand? What are they saying?

## MONITOR CONVERSATIONS

Once you know where your audiences are, it's essential to stay involved by regularly monitoring what's being said. You can set up tools—such as Google Alerts or Technorati Favorites—that allow you to track these conversations effectively on a daily basis.

## JOIN THE CONVERSATION

But remember, this is about demonstrating your brand promise and being authentic. It's not a monologue but a dialogue, so you have to act the same way online as you would in an offline relationship: honest and transparent to encourage people to share their thoughts. Engaging in two-way dialogue allows you to correct misinformation, raise interest and cultivate relationships.

## DRIVE INVOLVEMENT

This is the hard part. You want people interacting with you, not just reading your content. So you need to provide opportunities for participation. You can do this through collecting user-generated content, participating in interactive polls and contests, or moderating conversations. Develop a strategy for acknowledging and rewarding users' efforts and persistently seek new ways to drive engagement. That way, you strengthen users' bond to the brand and the brand community and, ultimately, create brand champions.

## CROWDSOURCE

Repurpose content that your followers, fans and blog posters generate. For example, you might use applications such as the Discussion Board on Facebook to initiate conversations around something specific to your business, and then repurpose this feedback to create more content—such as blog posts—to increase awareness and shape perceptions.

## MEASURE

You've listened, shared, connected and engaged—but is it

working? Putting measurements in place will help you track success back to your specific tactics. Aside from traditional measurement strategies (page visits, visit duration, new users, comments, links and referrals), you should also track your return on involvement. This means tracking actual engagement: response to questions, willingness to stay engaged over time and dialog between your organization and consumers. For a small business it's typically a qualitative measurement: Are you seeing more retweets, are you getting more questions/responses? After all, the goal of social media is to drive deeper engagement with your customers. Doing so will increase brand awareness, reinforce your brand promise, build loyalty, capture valuable customer insights, build your internal brand and contribute to new business opportunities.

## RE-EVALUATE YOUR COMMITMENT

Once you know the landscape, decide how much time is reasonably needed to accomplish your goals and assign the work to one or more people. The idea is to target your efforts where they'll be most effective and ignore the rest. Don't undercut your efforts by giving too little time—and give it time to work. Just like with any community, it takes personal investment to make it meaningful.

See, that wasn't so bad, was it? Is your SMFS improving?

# 16

# Drive Website Traffic Without Blurring Your Brand

## Use keywords your customers already use to hook customers, then deliver your unique value proposition.

Branding is all about differentiation—standing out in the customer's brain by being different than the competition. Search engine optimization is all about keywords, which identify what's already in a customer's brain about your category. So if your brand is expressed only in ways that make your difference clear, people aren't likely to find you through their initial keyword search.

So what's a savvy marketer supposed to do when driving prospects to your website has become job one? Does building your unique brand promise get pushed to job two?

The answer to this seeming paradox is, as always, to consider your customers. How will they search for your category?

What do they care about in relation to that? Does your brand suggest certain audience segments?

So if you're like Westhill Inc., a Seattle-based remodeling company whose brand centers on being "integrated home improvement experience managers" (focusing on the experience of home remodeling) and which targets upper-income women from 45 to 55, you wouldn't use "DIY" or "budget remodeling" as keywords. Instead, you would use "custom remodeling," "residential architects" or "design consultation." But you also wouldn't use "integrated home improvement experience managers," because no one is searching that way.

Instead, the way to get your brand value across is to start by thinking about the terms your customers use, and then send searchers to landing pages that act as the bridge from those generic keywords to your unique value. In other words, the landing page must pay off both in terms of the keyword, so they get what they were looking for, and your organization's unique approach to that keyword, so they get your differentiated value. It must feel like your brand, yet deliver on their expectations. You are, in essence, connecting the dots from keyword to unique value proposition.

When people search for "custom home remodeling," then click on Westhill's site, they arrive on a page that takes them from the generic concept of remodeling to Westhill's unique take on it: "We are a team of home improvement experience managers—designers, builders, client service specialists and home maintenance experts—dedicated to making your home improvement project exactly what you dreamed it would be."

In another example, Salal Credit Union targets health-care

workers in Puget Sound, Wash., and focuses on improving its members' financial health. But instead of using "financially healthy" as keywords for search optimization, it uses the more frequently searched "free checking accounts." That sends people to the credit union's website, where it pays off the financially healthy messaging. So visitors get what they were looking for, and more.

The fine line you have to walk is not to mislead with your SEO approach. That leads to fewer conversions and, ultimately, an SEO strategy that backfires and a slip in your rankings.

As John Lincoln of SEO Inc. says in a recent blog post, "In SEO, just like in life, honesty is the best policy. If you try to cut corners by not thoroughly thinking through an SEO strategy that makes sense for both the website users and the search engines, your site will suffer.

"You must have keywords in the right places, you must engage in some type of link-building, and you have to optimize your site with best practices. But without considering what your customers want, giving them the information they need and making sticky, popular pages, your site will never reach greatness." I would add: You will never build your unique, distinct and valuable brand.

# Part Three

# Branding in Real Life

Marketing is the talk. Your employees are the walk. So to walk the talk, you have to make sure your employees are educated and motivated to consistently deliver on your brand's promise. At every touch point lies an opportunity to create an experience; so here are a few ideas for getting your team up to speed on your brand and inspiring them to create some brand-defining experiences of their own.

# 17

# Branding Starts With Your Employees

## They need to know how to deliver the brand experience to your customers. Get them on board.

Branding externally is where most companies focus. But branding needs to start with your employees, because they are the ones delivering your brand experience. They need to understand what makes your organization better and different, and be guided to make decisions that increase that beneficial difference. That comes from internal branding.

The goal of internal branding is to help all employees understand how their roles positively impact the customer experience. This is true for every firm, no matter how small. It may be easier to impart your story and values in a small company, but you still need to do it. Here are the five components of a successful internal branding initiative. Together, they help you define, live and deliver your brand promise:

## BRAND TOOLS

These are what the organization uses to guide all decision-making, behavior and communications. How you describe your brand difference must be actionable, so employees know how the brand influences the way they make decisions. In companies with the most successful brands, their top-level business strategy is also a brand tool, sometimes called a strategic role. The **strategic role** describes why a prospective customer must consider the company. So while Home Depot could have said it was a big hardware store, instead, it framed its role in the market as the resource center for the do-it-yourselfer, and aligned its services and people behind that role.

The **guiding principle** is a company's unique approach to its strategic role. It's not a message—it's every employee's compass for making on-the-job decisions. For Group Health Credit Union, the guiding principle is connecting, coupled with a strategic role of money management made easy. "Connecting" means that every Group Health Credit Union employee looks for ways to form relationships with its members.

Other useful brand tools include positioning, values, cultural norms and personality. Together, these tools act as the compass for employee actions and communications. But they won't work without . . .

## CULTURE AND LEADERSHIP

The corporate culture includes the heritage, language, values, corporate structure and events unique to the company. It's essential that the leadership continually demonstrates and talks about the corporate culture as part of the internal branding process.

Two brand tools that can help managers build the culture are **cultural norms** and **personality**. Cultural norms are values in action. One example: "Since we reward initiative, I've set up meetings with three potential partners this week." You can discover what norms currently exist through querying employees with such questions as, "What are the unwritten rules for getting ahead in our organization?"

The **brand personality** is a series of traits that sets the standard for how employees treat each other and the world, as well as the tone and manner of company communications. Which leads us to . . .

## BRAND MANAGEMENT

Even in smaller companies, I don't recommend treating internal branding as a series of one-off, unrelated tactics such as holding an employee brand event or conducting an employee marketing campaign. Rather, use a systematic approach that begins by determining who will be responsible for the brand work and what the priorities for building the brand will be in year one. Which brings us to . . .

## THE CHANGE PLAN

Branding is an evolving process. Your employees add to it every day. The change plan describes how the organization will move from Point A to Point B. While it will cover the logistics of internal branding, such as brand strategy priorities and performance guidelines, it is most concerned with change management: helping people move through the transition cycle, beginning with denial and ending with acceptance for any change. Once the cycle is complete, it will begin again—your goal is to make a continual impact on the brand. And how you know you do that is through . . .

## BRAND MEASUREMENT

The very best internal branding will fail if it isn't tied to clear measurements. I recommend several indicators associated with employee commitment. Employee commitment, in turn, results in less turnover, greater word-of-mouth recommendation, positive brand awareness and greater productivity. Employee brand strength measurements include:

- Participation in your online brand community
- Willingness to recommend your organization to others as a place to work or to buy products
- Willingness to work for you for less money than that employee would accept from competitors
- Buy-in to your future business direction
- Ability to accurately explain your brand promise and apply it to his or her work.

So in your enthusiasm to build a strong brand to gain more loyal customers, don't neglect the people building that strong brand—and start your branding process from the inside out.

# 18

# Beyond Brand Definition

## Defining your brand is easy. Living up to that promise—from your invoices to your office decor—is harder.

After brand definition . . . then what?

More and more, companies are realizing they must actively manage their brand promise in the market, first by defining it, then by communicating it and living it.

The brand definition process is fairly well accepted: It involves qualitative, in-depth interviews with customers and internal staff on the value an organization brings to the market, followed by an analysis of the data to develop a series of conceptual tools that define the brand. These tools become the filter for actions and decisions so that employees are clear on how to deliver on the brand's promise.

But too many times, companies go through an expensive and time-consuming branding process only to snap back to old habits. The advertising agency creates flashy creative instead of a campaign that clearly demonstrates the company's differentiation. A new vice president of marketing wants to bring a fresh approach with an "updated message" that fails to communicate how the company is living its brand. Or senior management forgets that one of its primary jobs is to use the brand as a strategic driver in developing new products and services and to guide mergers and acquisitions. As a result, employees stop using the brand tools to guide their own actions and decisions. Then you're back to square one.

Defining your brand is the easy part. Using your brand to drive actions and communications is much harder, because it requires new behaviors.

Here are five actions to take to make sure your organization lives its brand:

## BRAINSTORM

Get your team together and brainstorm five new things to do to live your brand, five things to stop doing and five things to do more of. A health-care clinic decided to upgrade its waiting room to align it with a brand promise of being welcoming; a smoothie shop decided to welcome all returning customers by name to demonstrate its brand promise of "making a personal connection."

## BRAND-AT-A-GLANCE

Create a brand-at-a-glance one-page document that outlines your brand promise and informs employees and vendors how to use the brand as a filter for decisions and communications. You can make this a laminated card, a screen saver, a magnet or include it in your employee handbook.

## HIRING ON BRAND

Work your brand promise into your hiring, reviews and reward systems, so people know they will be measured by how well they live the brand. When hiring, make sure you ask questions that tell you whether the candidate can treat customers the way your brand promises. Your review process also has to make sure that it judges employees' work, at least in part, by how well they have demonstrated your company's promise.

## CONTINUALLY REINFORCE

Use company meetings and e-mails to reinforce how a big contract, win or initiative reflects your brand promise. Make the case for how change (in the form of an articulated brand promise) will make your employees' lives and careers better. Some company presidents start each weekly meeting with an anecdote about how the company demonstrated living its brand that week.

## CUSTOMER TOUCH-POINT AUDIT

Do a customer touch-point audit to determine how well every customer contact and communication is delivering on your stated brand promise. I guarantee this will be eye-opening. One of my clients discovered that its invoices were entirely contradictory to its brand promise of "respectful."

Larger organizations may need the help of a change management consultant to get people, processes and infrastructures in alignment with the ability to deliver on a newly articulated brand promise. But smaller, entrepreneurial companies typically can do it on their own. The important thing is to not leave living your brand up to chance, but to manage your brand promise delivery as well as you manage your receivables.

# 19

# Unintentional Leadership

## What you think you're modeling isn't always what people pick up. Here's what employees say they've learned from me.

When you're running a company, you try to model the best behaviors and get people thinking about ways to build the company's brand. So I praise for the behaviors I like, try to exemplify a good work ethic and strategic thinking, reward integrity and learning, and look for ways to manage to the triple bottom line. But what you think you're modeling isn't always what people pick up.

With that in mind, I decided to conduct an experiment. I asked my employees to tell me what their biggest "aha" moments have been; what have they learned while working at Parker LePla? I thought I knew what their answers would be. I was wrong. And their answers reflect the true brand we are living vs. my intentions.

It turns out that leadership can be an unintentional act. Here are some of the things my employees say I'm demonstrating even when I don't know I'm doing it:

### "HOW CAN I SIMPLIFY THAT EVEN FURTHER?"

We're branding wonks here, fascinated by the intellectual challenges and theoretical concepts of branding. But our clients are not. We need to strip away all the complexity of our grandiose ideas to get to the simple yet powerful truths that help our clients be more of who they are.

### ORGANIZATIONAL BUY-IN OF AN IDEA IS AS IMPORTANT AS THE IDEA ITSELF

I had this insight late in the game: I'm great at the idea part and less good at follow-through and implementation. The key to implementation is getting stakeholders excited about it so they will follow through on the promise of the brand. It is the client who has to deliver on his or her company's brand promise day in and day out. Without the structure and enthusiasm in place for that to happen, any branding exercise will fail.

### GREAT IDEAS COME FROM COLLABORATION

Anytime I'm stuck, I bring in the team for a brainstorm. The results are always fun, better than I could do myself—and every teammember leaves with more energy.

### RECOGNITION MAKES A BIG DIFFERENCE TO EMPLOYEES

We have institutionalized recognition and appreciation when we literally give kudos to each other at the end of our weekly staff meetings. This fosters a culture of appreciation and sure feels good, both in the giving and the receiving of kudos. It's part of our internal brand.

### DON'T DWELL ON YOUR MISTAKES

Learn from them and move on. We're not fear-based here. Mistakes are inevitable because we're only human. When mistakes happen, the questions are: How fast do you take responsibility for them, how completely can you fix them, and how much did you learn from them?

### IF YOU SAY IT CONFIDENTLY, PEOPLE WILL BELIEVE YOU

Isn't that the secret of all consulting, right there in a nutshell?

Because your people live your brand, it's important to be aware of what you're modeling. What are your employees learning from what you say, what you model—and what you're not even aware of? It's a good idea to find out so you can do more of the good stuff and strengthen your brand delivery.

# 20

# On-Brand Employees for On-Brand Companies

## Here's how to hire the employees who can deliver on your promise to your customers.

We are now several months into a tentative growth cycle in the economy, and that means some of us, for the first time in two years, are thinking about hiring. For a small business, hiring decisions can be a make-it or break-it issue. One compulsive liar, professional victim or weak link in skills can bring down a business when there are just a few of you. If your company is bigger, that kind of person can bring down morale. Even someone who's just operating at a different level than everyone else can have a huge negative impact. So it's important to hire well.

Many organizations just consider role, skill and presentation when hiring. That leaves out the all-important aspect of whether the prospective employee can deliver your brand promise, day in and day out.

If your communications are on-brand, that's great. But if your people aren't delivering what you're promising, you're on the road to oblivion. The secret to creating a strong brand isn't great advertising, but how well your employees deliver on your promise. In fact, you can make a case that great advertising without great brand delivery will kill your company faster, because the disconnect between what you promise and what you actually do will be big enough to chase away customers and create negative word-of-mouth.

Every employee needs to understand and be able to act and interact in ways that create satisfied, committed customers. They need to be able to project your company's unique personality and make decisions that will move your company toward a bigger brand difference in the marketplace. They need to deliver the brand as part of their jobs, every day. So how do you hire "on-brand"?

Here are a few tips for finding, screening and hiring potential brand champions:

## DESCRIBE YOUR BRAND PROMISE

Then, describe your ideal employee. These descriptions will help you create a list of desired characteristics, questions to ask and scenarios to pose in an interview. While brand clarity alone won't scare away the wrong candidates and attract the right ones, it will help. The Mayo Clinic, which has a strong team ethos, typically doesn't hire superstar doctors because their ambitions are at odds with the clinic's brand of teamwork. Those in hospitality industries know they need to hire people who value relationships, because strong hospitality brands need employees who enhance the guest experience.

## USE EXISTING EMPLOYEES FOR REFERRALS

A referral reflects on the person making it, so people are careful about whom they recommend. In addition, your employees are in the best position to determine whether someone they know will be able to deliver on your brand promise.

## USE YOUR HIRING PROCESS TO SCREEN FOR SPECIFIC TRAITS IMPORTANT TO YOUR COMPANY'S BRAND

For example, Cold Stone Creamery has applicants sing or show off their talent in a three-minute session called "bust a move." If teamwork is central to your company, ask for examples of where being on a team worked, and where it didn't. Since great writing skills are a necessity at our firm, we always ask for an unusual cover letter. We tell candidates to treat their cover letter like a personal branding exercise; an opportunity to demonstrate their personality, to tell us what it is that makes them unique and how they can be asset to our team. So the framework is loose, and we look to see how they make themselves stand out from the crowd—from clever storytelling or writing about their assets in the form of a poem to sending a video that demonstrates their skills. That helps us gauge writing style and ability. It also determines how creative applicants are, whether they can follow directions and how closely they pay attention to details.

## USE THE COMPANY'S PERSONALITY TRAITS TO DRIVE THE INTERVIEW PROCESS

If you are leading-edge, make sure your people are, too. If you are friendly, hire friendly people. If you are hip, hire hipsters. If part of your brand promise is "fun," for example, don't hire an introvert in a customer-facing position. And beware of mimickers—people who pick up on the expectation but can't walk the talk. We always ask candidates to give an example of when they've used a particular attribute to solve a problem.

After you've hired the on-brand employee, you still have work to do.

- You have to orient employees to your brand difference, training them how to make decisions using the brand as a compass.
- You have to train them to be brand storytellers and to think about delivering a brand experience in everything they do.
- You have to measure and reward people for demonstrating on-brand behaviors.
- You have to model brand-based behavior yourself. If your brand is about trustworthiness and you tell your receptionist to tell people you're out when you're not, that's giving employees a mixed message about living your brand.

I didn't say it would be easy—it's not. But the best way to create a strong brand is through your people. And the best way to do that is in the hiring process.

# 21

# Are You a Brand?

## Yes, you have a personal brand, so make sure it reflects what you stand for.

After no requests for the topic for years, I've been asked to speak on "personal branding" twice in the past month. Because I pay attention to what the universe seems to want me to do, I'm taking notice. So do I have anything to add to the topic? Is personal branding something to pay attention to, as the universe suggests?

My kneejerk reaction is along the lines of Maureen Johnson's BlogHer manifesto: I am not a brand! You can't put people in boxes; we are more than what we say about ourselves, etc. But if I apply my definition of a brand, "the promise that you keep," then I know that we all live our brand promise in everything we do, and that understanding and articulating that promise helps us be more of the person we intend to be, not less. I also know that our personal brand as it applies to our business selves is one expression of our whole self, and requires more conscious molding.

For insight, I've drawn on the lessons learned from the way we help companies figure out their brand promise. For businesses, we do research with customers and employees to determine the meaning behind their brand, then articulate it through a set of actionable brand tools. Here's how we would adapt this process for personal branding, one that honors your individuality and complexity. The goal is to articulate the following: What sets you apart? What are your passions? What are your greatest strengths? What can people expect from you?

The first step is to ask three good friends for the top three adjectives they would use to describe you. Write down what you think your top three descriptors are, as well. Is there consistency? Figure out what they say about you and understand the personal story that weaves those things together within you.

Secondly, Google yourself, to see if the world's view of you maps to your self-image. (A friend told me to Google image myself one day, and I was surprised—and horrified—to discover that I came up second, after a very graphic picture of a part of female anatomy an obstetrician named Lynn Parker uses in her PowerPoint on rare female syndromes. Not exactly the first impression I want to give people. ) Your online footprint is what you're currently telling the world you stand for, so it's important to know what's out there.

Third, write down the value you think you bring to the world. Some people do this in the form of a mission statement, but that feels contrived to me. Instead, I like to encapsulate personal brands in a set of two or three adjectives that hold some action as well as stable qualities. My brand is around creativity and laughter. My husband's is around loyalty and obsession (in a good way). My partner Briana's is around balance and insight. My partner Joe's is around listening and strategy.

So what do you do with this brand description once you're written it down?

## BE CONSISTENT

Live that brand in everything you do over time. Look at all your customer touchpoints. Know that everything matters—what you do, what you say, how you present yourself, what you choose to spend your time and energy on. I hired an image consultant to tell me about the first impression I give off, and how to improve it. When I did this (painful, but useful), I made a few tweaks to my clothes, hair and accessories that improved my ability to be heard by clients. (OK, I'll never be good at this part, but at least I'm trying!)

## USE WORD-OF-MOUTH MARKETING

Use word-of-mouth marketing to share your value with others (a tactic otherwise known as networking). Identify a specific, targeted audience to form good, solid relationships with. You will find more value in that rather than marketing to the masses. Join a group, and go deep.

## USE YOUR BRAND TO INFORM HOW YOU SHOW UP PUBLICLY

Use your profile on LinkedIn, Facebook and Twitter, as well as your blog, website and other tools, to strengthen your brand. Pay attention to what you are posting. Before you put something on the web, think about how that affects your personal brand and how your audience will perceive you.

So is personal branding hype or important? If your brand is the promise you keep, then we all have a brand already. The real question isn't "should you have a personal brand?" but "how do you live it"?